Milly and Her Kittens

Written by Barbara A. Wilson
Illustrated by Aron Fine

Item # F2SMILL1 ISBN 978-1-56778-542-5

PUBLISHED BY:

Wilson Language Training Corporation
47 Old Webster Road
Oxford, MA 01540
United States of America

(800) 899-8454 | www.wilsonlanguage.com

Printed in the U.S.A.   August 2016

Milly is a cat who has
a big job on her hands.

She just had six kittens!
My, my! That is a lot of kittens!

Here is Kip.
Kip is a tan kitten.

Here is Jeb.
Jeb is a black kitten.

Here is Sid.
Sid is a black kitten, too.

There are three kittens that are black and tan. They are Penny, Teddy, and Tom.

Milly has a big job.

Jeb and Sid fell off the bench.

Kip is in the box.

Penny and Teddy
went down the hall.

Tom is lost. "My, my!"
said Milly. "Where is Tom?"

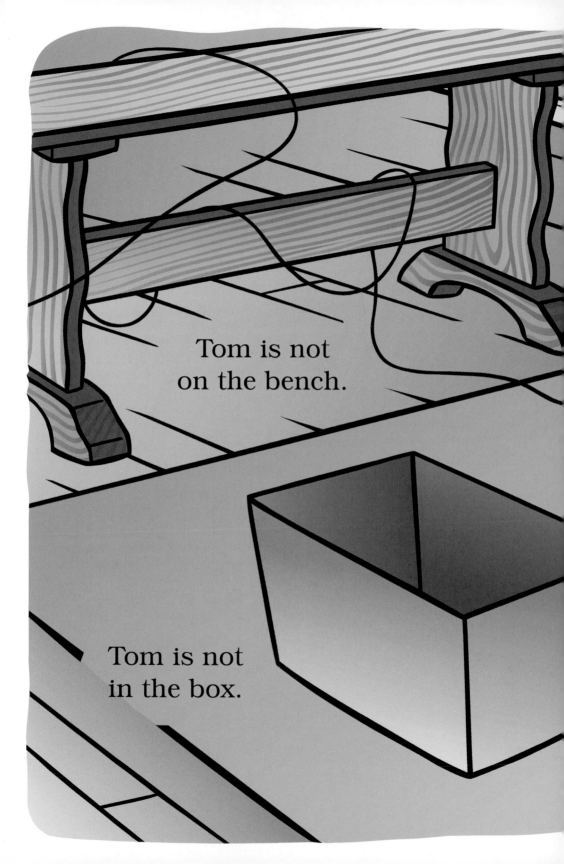

Tom is not
down the hall.

There he is! Tom is not lost.
Tom is in the big red bin.

At last, Milly has
all her kittens back.

She is a glad mom.